This Bing book belongs to:

....

Bracknell Forest Borough Council	
5430000072898 9	
Askews & Holts	2017

The Bing television series is created by Acamar Films and Brown Bag Films and adapted from the original books by Ted Dewan

Based on the script by Lead Writers Matthew Leys and Lucy Murphy and Team Writers
Mikael Shields, Philip Bergkvist and Ted Dewan

Edited by Stella Gurney
Designed by Anna Lubecka

First published in the UK in 2017 by HarperCollins Children's Books.
HarperCollins Children's Books is a division of HarperCollins Publishers Ltd, 1 London Bridge Street, London, SE1 9GF

1 3 5 7 9 10 8 6 4 2

978-0-00-818303-5

MIX
Paper from
responsible sources
FSC® C007454

FSC ™ is a non-profit international organisation established to promote the responsible management of the world's forests. Products carrying the FSC label are independently certified to assure consumers that they come from forests that are managed to meet the social, economic and ecological needs of present and future generations, and other controlled sources.

Find out more about HarperCollins and the environment at
www.harpercollins.co.uk/green

Paddling Pool

HarperCollins *Children's Books*

Round the corner,
not far away,
Bing is going
paddling today.

"Sula-a-aaa! Come on Sula! It's me!"

"Well hello," says Amma, opening the door. "Someone's in a hurry!"

"Yes, me!" says Bing. "We're going to the paddling pool – and Sula's coming too!"

"Here I am, Bing!" laughs Sula.
"And I've got a new bouncy ball!
I'm going to play with it in the
water and go SPLASH!"

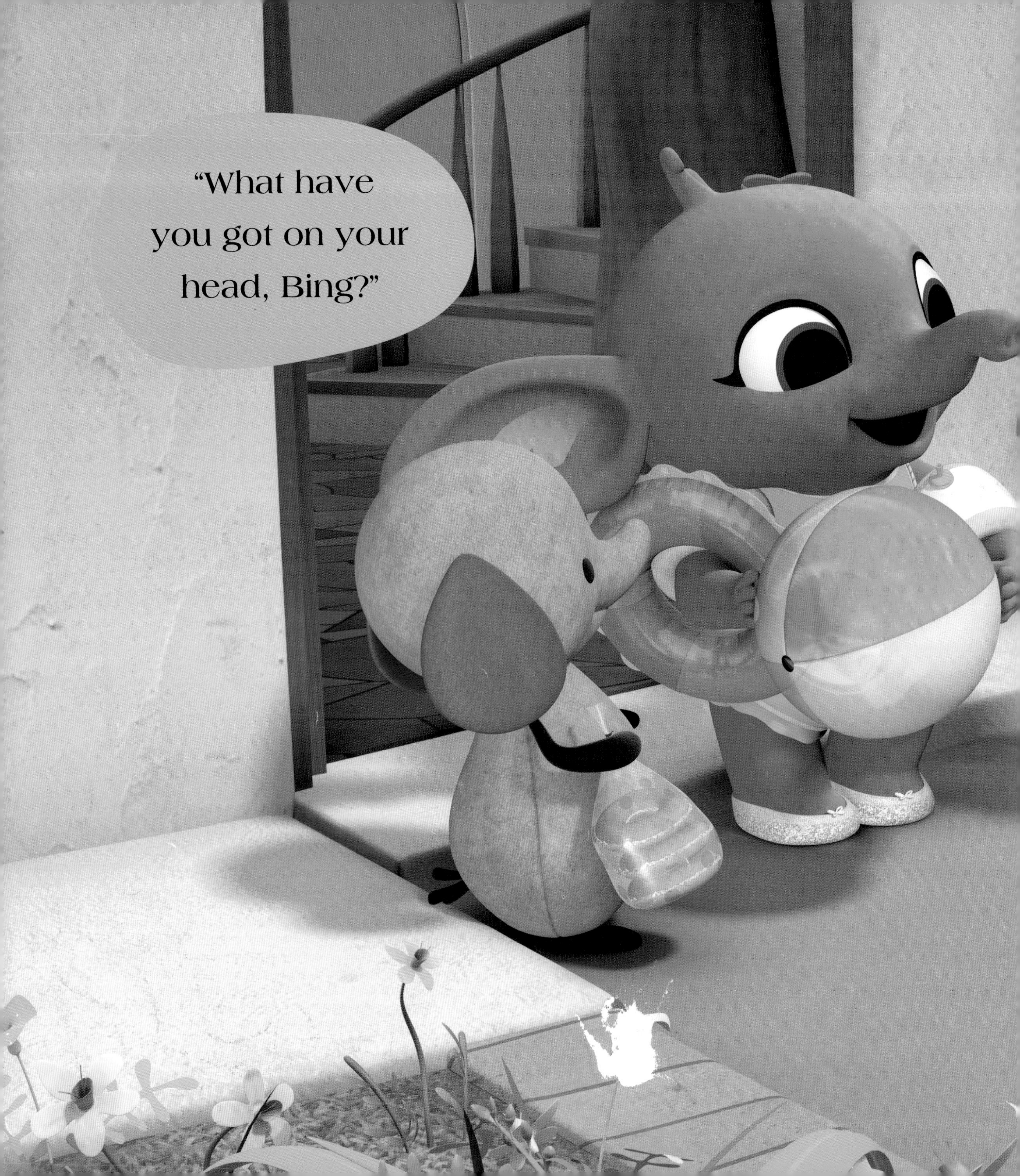
"What have you got on your head, Bing?"

"My blue goggles," says Bing. "And Flop's got a yummy picnic."

Indeed!

"Ooh - what's in the **picnic**, Flop?"

"Well, let's see...

We've got juice drinks...

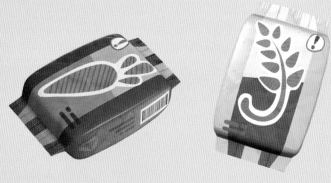 some grapes...

yummy biscuits..."

"And I have made some carroty bagels!" says Amma.

"Oh - thank you, Amma!"

Bing, Sula and Flop set off down the path. But then...

"Wait a minute!"
calls Amma from the door.

"Remember, that paddling pool is busy-busy! So make sure you can **always** see Flop, and he can see you!"

"OK Amma!
See you later!"

"Waaaait a minute!"

"Ohhh – what is it, Amma?" cries Sula.

"No running in the pool."

"OK Amma!" says Sula. "Come on, Bing - let's go!"

"Waaaait a minute!"

"What is it, Amma?" groans Sula.

"Most important of all," smiles Amma... "no pee-pee in the pool."

"I would **never** pee-pee in the water!" giggles Sula.

"Er... and I won't," promises Bing.

Let's gooooooooooo!

"I love the paddling pool!" says Sula. "I'm going to **splash** my ball when I get there."

"And I'm going to wear my **blue goggles**," says Bing.

"Ha ha Sula, you're all blue!

EVERYthing's blue!

That's funny!"

Bing, Sula and Flop arrive at the
paddling pool. Outside, they
see a **sign** with four little pictures on it.

"What does the sign say, Flop?"

"Well, the first picture says you can't **splash** your **ball** in the pool," says Flop.

"Awww!" says Sula.

"This one means **no running** in the pool."

"Because it's slippy," says Bing.

"And this one means **no eating**," says Flop.

"But what about our picnic, Flop?" asks Bing.

"We won't eat our picnic in the pool, silly. All the carroty bagels would go soggy," giggles Sula.

"I know what the last one says, Flop!" smiles Bing. "No pee-pee in the pool!" Everybody laughs.

"OK!" says Flop. "Are we ready?"

Let's go, go, go, go, goooo!

"Where is everybody?"

"There's no water, Flop!"

"Hmm, it seems the pool hasn't been filled up."

"But it's no fun like this," cries Bing.
"We can't do anything."

"Well - are you sure?" asks Flop.
"The water's not here today, but the pool is."
Sula's ball falls into the empty pool.

It bounces...

and Bing runs
to fetch it.

Boing-boing!

"NO Bing!" calls Sula.
"You can't splash the
ball in the pool!"

"But I'm not doing splashing, Sula!" laughs Bing. "Because there's **no water!**"

"What about running, Flop?" asks Sula.

"Well," smiles Flop. "You can't slip if there isn't any water."

Boing!

"I love the paddling pool like this!" shouts Bing.

"Now," says Flop, "Where shall we have our picnic?"

"Let's have it in the pool!"

Yummy!

Hi!

Me and Sula went to the **paddling pool.**

Sula brought her bouncy ball...

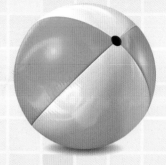

...and I wore my **blue goggles.**

But when we got there, all the water was

gone!

And we were sad.

But Flop said we could **still play** in the pool...

...**and** we even had our **picnic** in it.

If you can't do what you want to do, you can do **a different** thing and sometimes it's **better.**

Playing in an empty paddling pool...

it's a Bing thing.